This book belongs to

DATE DUE

Demco, Inc. 38-293

Rabén & Sjögren Stockholm

Library of Congress catalog card number: PZ7.S96917 [E]--dc 19 87-28355
Originally published in Sweden under the title
Maja tittar på naturen by Rabén & Sjögren, 1983
First American edition, 1988
Third printing 1992
Printed in Italy

R & S Books are distributed in the United States of America by Farrar, Straus and Giroux, New York;
in the United Kingdom by Ragged Bears, Andover; in Canada by Methuen Publications, Toronto, Ontario;
and in Australia by ERA Publications, Adelaide

ISBN 91 29 58786 7

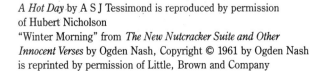

NICKY
THE NATURE DETECTIVE

pictures by Lena Anderson

text by Ulf Svedberg

translated by Ingrid Selberg

R&S
BOOKS

Stockholm   New York   Toronto   London   Adelaide

This is Nicky. All through the year, she loves to explore the changes in nature. There's so much to look for and discover. All you need is a good pair of eyes and ears.

In the spring, the birds sing; in the summer, there are hundreds of plants and insects (it's hard to keep track of them all); in the autumn, Nicky watches the migrating birds and looks for fruits and mushrooms. Only in winter does nature quiet down, but there's still lots to see.

Try keeping track of one special tree. Nicky has picked a red maple. It is one of the most common trees in North America and grows everywhere from Quebec, Canada, to southern Florida and west to eastern Texas. Its leaves turn beautiful colors in the autumn. Choose whatever tree you find most interesting and go out exploring, just like Nicky.

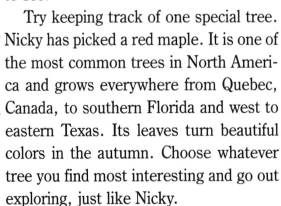

There's much more to nature than you think. You can investigate the plants and animals themselves, as well as their tracks and the other clues they leave behind; feathers, perhaps a mouse skeleton, a gnawed-up pinecone, or an unusual flower.

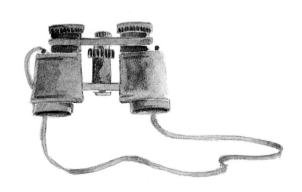

But Nicky can't show you everything — only a little bit of what she finds especially interesting.

Field guides to flowers and birds are very useful, and if you can get a pair of binoculars or a magnifying glass, they are a great help, too.

At the back of the book, there's a list of books you can read if you want to learn more. They might tell you why birches grow witches'-brooms, how the crossbill breeds in the middle of winter, and if the earwig can really crawl into a person's ear. But first, have a good time with Nicky!

AND YOUR EARS TOO...

SPRING

This is the weather the cuckoo likes,
    And so do I;
When showers betumble the chestnut
    spikes,
    And nestlings fly:
And the little brown nightingale bills his
    best,
And they sit outside at 'The Travellers'
    Rest',
And maids come forth sprig-muslin drest,
And citizens dream of the south and west,
    And so do I.

Thomas Hardy

TREES

The maple tree flowers in early spring, and insects gather to suck the sweet nectar from the maple blossoms. The leaf buds usually burst open a few days later, and the pale green leaves appear. The winged maple fruits or "helicopters" (they are called samaras) mature four to six weeks later.

BIRDS

The birds are singing and preparing their new homes. It takes most birds three to nine days to build a nest. Some birds have more than one brood a summer, and they'll build a new nest for each set of young. The male wren builds several dummy nests, and his female companion choses one to lay her eggs in.

PLANTS

The celandine has almost finished blooming when the wood anemone appears, like a white carpet. In the evening, the wood anemone closes its petals. Nicky tries an experiment to see if this is true. She puts an empty tin over a few open wood anemones for half an hour. It is dark inside the can, so the flowers are tricked into thinking it's evening. Half an hour later, when Nicky checks, the flowers have closed their petals.

INSECTS

The few butterflies that Nicky can see in springtime have spent the winter in tree crevices or in lofts and cellars. Most butterflies die in the autumn after laying their eggs. The eggs, and sometimes the larvae, can survive the winter. Ants start to tidy up their anthills for the summer.

OTHER ANIMALS

The racoon gives birth to its young in a tree den. Young racoons twitter like birds when their nest is disturbed. Racoons climb easily and prefer to live in trees, but their dens can also be found in abandoned buildings or on the ground. Racoons will eat anything, and they are very curious. People who live near the woods often discover that hungry racoons have investigated their garbage cans!

Trees

There are 750 kinds of trees (species) in North America. Some are tall and straight, like the Douglas fir; others are gnarled and twisted, like the bristle-cone pine. Trees which lose their leaves in the winter are called deciduous. Most native North American trees are deciduous. Trees, such as pines, which keep their leaves all year are called evergreens.

The leaves grow in spring. They make food for the tree with sunlight, air, and water. If you break a twig, a bit of liquid called sap oozes out. The tree is "bleeding." The sap from sugar maples becomes the maple syrup that you eat on pancakes.

Most sunlight comes from the south. Trees often grow leaning southward, and their annual rings are wider on the south side.

A tree's history is written in its annual rings. In good years, the rings are wider; the tree has grown more.

Willow twigs take root easily in water. Nicky puts some in a jar and changes the water often. When the little root hairs have sprouted, she looks at them with a magnifying glass.

What's underneath the bark?
Pick away a small piece of bark on a dead tree or stump. You'll find lots of creepy crawlies hiding underneath — millipedes, spiders, small beetles, and ants. You can see patterns of tunnels made by insects in the wood itself.

NORTH

SOUTH

I CAN SEE YOU HAVE EXPERIENCED A GREAT DEAL

6

The bark protects living trees from insects and disease. The giant sequoias of Sierra Nevada in California have bark up to sixty centimeters (two feet) wide. Not even forest fires can harm those trees!

How old can a tree get?
Trees have long lives. Smaller deciduous trees live from forty to fifty years. The Great Basin bristle-cone pine can live up to four thousand years.

How tall can a tree grow?
Giant sequoias and coastal redwoods can grow up to 110 meters (360 feet).

Listen to the pinecones!
On a quiet winter day, Nicky can hear the pinecones popping. The seeds inside the cone are ripe. When released, they sail off on little wings. They land close by, and new pine trees start to grow.

How cones grow
Conifers have both male and female flowers. Pollen from the yellow male flower is carried by the wind and lands on the red female flower. It then grows into a green cone. When the cone is ripe, it turns brown. The scales open and the seeds are released.

CAN YOU HEAR THE PINECONES?

Why do birds sing?

ZEE IT, ZEE IT...

HEAVENLY!

Doesn't it sound lovely? thinks Nicky. But when a bird sings, it's really a courtship song. A male is trying to attract females into his territory.

When the male has found a partner, they mate and build a nest. The male still sings, but now it's to warn off other males: Keep away!

When the young have hatched, he stops singing. He doesn't want to attract any other animals to the nest. The young need to be protected.

How old do birds become?

A bird lives a dangerous life. It can be eaten by an enemy, get caught in bad weather, starve, become ill, or fail to breed. Even if it survives these dangers, it doesn't grow very old. A little bird, such as a robin, or sparrow, lives only about three years. The bigger the bird, the longer it tends to live.

8

The inhabitants of the nesting box

In spring, birds give their nesting box a good cleaning. Both the male and the female help. When the nest is ready, the male sits outside, singing, and sometimes he helps the female sit on her eggs. (This varies a bit, depending on the bird.) Small birds sit on their eggs for about three weeks before they hatch. The male brings food for the female and later for the chicks, too. They need feeding many times an hour. If you're lucky, you might see the chicks leaving the nesting box. Afterwards, they stay nearby and beg for food from their parents.

The cuckoo

The cuckoo doesn't always build its own nest. Sometimes the female lays her eggs in another bird's nest. The foster bird never notices a thing.

The cuckoo's egg develops more quickly than the foster parents' own eggs. When the cuckoo chick hatches, it shoves the other eggs and young out of the nest. The foster parents don't notice even if their own young are lying on the ground underneath the nest and cheeping.

The foster parents work very hard to feed the young cuckoo. It grows quickly and gets big. Sometimes the tiny parent has to sit on the young cuckoo's back to stuff food into its mouth.

Sleeping birds don't fall down

Birds don't fall off branches when they sleep. Their toes grip the branch automatically. There is a tendon that "locks" the foot into place.

...FIFTEEN ... SIXTEEN... SEVENTEEN

9

The Frog,

Spring is the heyday of the frog. In March and April, you can hear their croaking from ponds and ditches. The male grasps a female and clambers onto her back, while other males try to push him off.

The eggs are fertilized at the same moment as the female lays them in the water. They are covered with a jelly that swells up so that each egg looks like a round ball. After a few days, you can see something black inside the egg. This is the tadpole.

About three weeks later, there are small fishlike tadpoles with gills swimming about. The tadpoles grow quickly; their gills disappear and are replaced by lungs. They grow hind legs, followed by front legs. All the legs have webs between the toes. The tail shrinks and

Hello!

the tadpole has become a little frog. It is ready to leave the water and live on land.

Many animals — water shrews, fish, some birds and snakes — love to eat frogs!

You can tell the difference between frogs' eggs, or spawn, and toad spawn. Frogs lay their eggs in clumps, while toads lay theirs in long, winding ribbons.

What do frogs eat?

Tiny tadpoles scrape off algae growing on water plants. Larger tadpoles eat bits of the plants themselves and dead animals. Grown frogs like insects, earthworms, snails, and even tadpoles! They are also good at catching flies with their long, sticky tongues.

Raise a frog

Take a large bowl or aquarium. Place a layer of clean sand on the bottom and add some pond water. Anchor some water plants in the sand with small stones. Put in a little frog spawn. When the tadpoles hatch, feed them lettuce and nettle leaves. Remember to change the water once in a while, and return the frogs to the pond when their legs begin to appear. They grow very quickly.

Toads

don't jump like frogs. They crawl. Their skin is rough, with warts on it, whereas frogs have smooth skin. Nicky can easily tell them apart.

Snakes

don't have ears, but they can feel vibrations in the ground when someone is coming. Then they slither away. Grass and glass snakes are completely harmless. Nicky leaves all snakes alone. They are useful because they hunt shrews and mice.

Look at the frog

FIRST AN EGG...   THEN A TADPOLE...   THAT GROWS LEGS...   ITS TAIL SHRINKS...   ALL COMPLETE! UP ON LAND!

Flowers

The flower

To our eyes, most flowers are beautifully colored, but insects see them differently. Inside the flower is the pistil and stamen, which are necessary for the plant to reproduce itself.

The leaves

All green plants can make their own food. Using water from the soil, carbon dioxide from the air, sunshine and chlorophyll (the green substance in the leaves), they make a nutritious sugar and oxygen.

WHEN YOU PICK A FLOWER, DON'T PULL IT UP BY THE ROOTS OR THERE MIGHT NOT BE ANY NEXT YEAR!

The stalk

lifts the leaves and flowers up to the light. It stands up against bad weather and wind, even if it looks spindly.

The roots

hold the plant firmly in the ground and also draw up nutrients (minerals) from the soil with their fine hairs.

12

and Bees

HERE ARE THE GRAINS OF POLLEN

Just think of all the flowers there are and all their lovely colors. Oddly enough, we are almost the only animals that can see those colors, and the plants don't care what we think. They just want to attract insects.

Insects don't see colors; they see ultraviolet light, which we can't see. Some plants have special signs to help flying insects find them. These signs show up in photographs taken in ultraviolet light.

Insects fly from flower to flower. Pollen sticks to their hairy bodies and a little of it brushes off on the next flower they visit. Only pollen from a cowslip can make another cowslip produce seeds.

Flowers attract insects with their nectar. Sometimes we say that bees and other insects are looking for honey, but really they are after nectar. They swallow the nectar and it is changed into honey inside a special honey stomach. Then the bee spits up the honey and stores it in a cell in the honeycomb. Nicky doesn't think it sounds too appetizing, but she likes brown bread and honey.

The bee brushes the grains of pollen off its body and makes them into a little ball stuck together with some honey. The pollen is stowed away between the hairs on the bee's hind legs, in the pollen basket. You can spot bees doing this if you keep your eyes open.

Bees are particularly fond of yellow colts-foot, celandine, fruit-tree blossoms, and oak flowers.

Some plants, such as pine trees, grasses, dandelions, and willow herbs, let the wind scatter their seeds.

In the spring, Nicky sometimes sneezes and sneezes. Her eyes run; her nose and throat itch. She has an allergy to pollen called hay fever. Many people are very sensitive to grass pollen and develop asthma or eczema.

YES, IT'S TRUE — BEES SPIT UP HONEY

13

I WONDER HOW LONG IT WILL TAKE...

When buds burst open

In the autumn, the horse chestnut stops growing. At the tip of each twig, there is a large pointed bud with a brown sticky covering. Sometime in April or May, the bud begins to open. The sticky covering, which protected the bud during the winter, leaves a scar on the twig when it falls off. See if you can spot them. You can tell how much a twig has grown in a year by the distance between the two scars. This is different from the "horseshoe" leaf scar.

Take a twig and place it in a jar filled with water, just as Nicky has done. You can do it with any type of tree, but the horse chestnut is especially good because it has large buds which are easy to see.

What happens to buds during the year?

Tie a little ribbon around a hazel, birch, oak, beech, or ash twig so that you can recognize it. Take a look at it regularly during the year until the tree loses its leaves. Draw it and measure how much it has grown.

Sow a seed

Plant some peas in plain soil in a flowerpot. (Yellow peas are good, but so are green peas or

THE BRANCHES WI
BOWS ON ARE MIN

14

runner beans.) Sow lots of them. Then it won't matter if you dig up one or two to have a look at the roots.

When a pea grows, it sucks up water and swells. The seed coat splits open and a little root emerges. The root comes first, and it grows downward to help hold the new plant in the soil.

In the tip of the root there is a cap which protects the sensitive tip from damage. Behind it lie lots of thin root hairs, which take up water

and minerals from the ground.

When the root is growing properly, the shoot begins to grow upward in the air. This shoot will become the stalk which carries the leaves and flowers and finally the fruit.

... IT WAS QUICKER THAN I THOUGHT!

15

How does the water reach the leaves?

Trees and flowers need lots of water to make their food. An average birch tree needs four hundred to six hundred liters (one hundred to one hundred and fifty gallons) of water every day during a warm summer.

But how does the water get from the roots to the top of a tall tree? Water comes up from the roots, through the trunk and along the branches to the leaves. The leaves are full of tiny holes through which the water evaporates and new water is constantly replacing the water that has evaporated.

AMAZING!

THE WATER-LILY TRICK

Try this trick of Nicky's. Pick a water-lily leaf with a long stalk. Place the leaf under water and blow through the stalk. The air will pass through the tiny holes in the leaf and make bubbles on the surface. If air can pass through these holes, so can water. Inside all plants, water moves through tiny tubes.

THE TULIP TRICK

Put a white tulip in a glass of water with some green (or other) food coloring in it. After a few hours, the tulip petals will have green streaks. The water has carried the coloring with it up into the flower.

THE LEAF TRICK

Tie a clear plastic bag around a leafy twig on a tree. Soon you will see drops of water inside the bag. This is water that has evaporated through the little holes in the leaves.

WATER AND FOOD COLORING

NOW WE'LL SOON SEE

17

SUMMER

A Hot Day

Cottonwool clouds loiter.
A lawnmower, very far,
Birrs. Then a bee comes
To a crimson rose and softly
Deftly and fatly crams
A velvet body in.

A tree, June-lazy, makes
A tent of dim green light.
Sunlight weaves in the leaves,
Honey-light laced with leaf-light,
Green interleaved with gold.
Sunlight gathers its rays
In sheaves, which the wind unweaves
And then reweaves — the wind
That puffs a smell of grass
Through the heat-heavy, trembling
Summer pool of air.

A. S. J. Tessimond

TREES

The maple's flowers have long since fallen off, and the leaves have turned dark green. You can hardly see the branches and twigs for all the leaves. Nicky loves to sit in the cool shade under her tree.

BIRDS

It's hard to see birds among all the greenery. Is there still one in the nesting box? Bluebirds or starlings may even have started a second brood of young.

PLANTS

Not all flowers are brightly colored. Many grasses have small, pale flower heads. In the meadows you may find daisies, clover, thistles, poppies, and buttercups. Nicky dries buttercups. They are still yellow and lovely in the wintertime. There are masses of dandelions — both flowers and seed heads — and Nicky picks the young leaves for salad.

INSECTS

The peacock and tortoiseshell butterflies settle on nettle leaves to lay their eggs because the caterpillars will eat those plants when they appear. Other insects are multiplying as well. The place is swarming with them.

OTHER ANIMALS

In the grass, you can hear shrews squeaking. They are always hungry. A shrew consumes more than its own weight in food daily, and it cannot live for more than a few hours without eating.

Buzzing, singing, chirping,

Insects make an incredible variety of sounds. Mosquitoes keep Nicky awake at night with their whining. But it's even worse when they are silent, because then she knows they're about to bite. Fat flies buzz in the sunlight on the porch, especially when there are cookies and juice on the table. Nicky tries to chase them away, but it isn't easy to kill a fly. They have compound eyes made up of many tiny eyes and can see movement more clearly than we can. They notice as soon as you get ready to strike a blow.

IF THE FLY WAS THIS SIZE, YOU COULD SEE ALL ITS COMPOUND EYES AND MOUTH PARTS CLEARLY

Flies are unpleasant and spread disease. They can be found wherever there is dung, dead animals, and excrement. The fly deposits saliva on its food. Set out a little bit of sugar and watch how the fly eats it. Its mouth is like a sucking pad that unfolds and works almost like a vacuum cleaner.

Mosquitoes lay their eggs in the water. When they hatch, the larvae stay near the surface of the water. But when there is danger, they swim down toward the bottom. In warm climates, mosquitoes can carry a dangerous disease called malaria.

In the summer, crickets and grasshoppers sing all day long. They live in the long grass and are at their loudest at the end of the summer, when the young ones join in.

Only the males sing. Grasshoppers rub their hind legs against their wing sheaths, and crickets rub their wing sheaths together. Different types have different songs, and you can learn to tell them apart. The females listen with interest. Their ears, by the way, are on their forelegs. But why not — flies have their sense of taste on their front feet!

How can you tell a grasshopper and a cricket apart? Grasshoppers have short antennae, and crickets have long ones. The female cricket has a long swordlike egg-laying tube.

THE CRICKET HAS LONG ANTENNAE...

20

and whining

... AND THE GRASSHOPPER HAS SHORT ANTENNAE

Bites and stings

Mosquitoes

The mosquito sucks blood with a tube which pierces the skin like a sharp needle. Only the female sucks blood; she needs it for her eggs to develop properly. Male mosquitoes stick to plant juices.

Mosquito bites usually itch. The mosquito injects a liquid into the blood which prevents it from clotting quickly. Don't kill the mosquito. Let it finish sucking. It will remove most of the liquid, and the bite won't itch as much.

Bees and wasps

Bee and wasp stings usually swell up. The bee has a sting in the tip of its abdomen. It looks

like two saws, with barbs and a dagger between the blades. The saws make a hole, and the knife sticks in and presses in the poison. The bee gets stuck, and when it flies away, the sting remains in the sore.

The wasp doesn't have such strong barbs on

its sting and can therefore pull it out again. The bee dies after stinging, but the wasp survives.

Ants

Ants also bite. The small red ants have a little sting with which they inject poison. The ordinary ant doesn't have a sting, but it can bite. It sprays formic acid with the tip of its abdomen, and the spurt can reach fifty centimeters (twenty inches) away. Hold your hand over the hill and smell!

GADFLY

Flies

There are some especially unpleasant flies that sting. In the summer, when it is warm and damp, horseflies, gadflies, midges, and gnats appear. They are so silent that you don't notice them until they bite.

Stinging nettles

Nettle leaves and stalks are covered with hairs with sharp tips. They break easily and the tip pierces the skin, injecting poisonous liquid. It stings but it isn't dangerous. Fresh young nettles make a delicious soup, but Nicky always wears gloves when picking them!

Most insect bites and stings only hurt for a short time, then the pain goes away. You can bathe the wound in ammonia or vinegar. It helps to rub raw onion on a bee sting, because the onion contains a substance that destroys bee poison. Try rubbing yourself with parsley to keep mosquitoes away.

GOT YOU!

23

Thousands of years ago, all plants were wild. Now we cultivate many of them for food: wheat, rye, maize, corn, oats, potatoes, and vegetables.

Wild plants are edible, too. But don't pick them along the roadside. They will be polluted by car exhaust.

WARNING!

Look everything up in a field guide so that you are *absolutely sure* you aren't eating anything poisonous. These berries are dangerous and should never be eaten: deadly nightshade, woody nightshade, and yew. Check them in your flower book.

IT'S LUCKY I BROUGHT MY FIELD GUIDE ALONG...

GOOD PLANTS

Elm The fruit of the elm tree tastes good in a green salad.

Silverweed grows on the beach. The young leaves can be eaten in a salad.

Dandelion leaves that grow in the dark (for example, under an old board) are especially delicious.

Cress comes in many varieties. Watercress is particularly tasty, but pick it only from fast-flowing streams.

Red clover The bees take the nectar, but we can gather the leaves and eat them in salad.

Yarrow The tiny, delicately lobed leaves can be used as a slightly bitter herb to put on food.

Polypody fern sometimes grows on old stone walls. Its root tastes like licorice.

you can eat

GOOD BERRIES

There are lots of good berries to eat, but there are also poisonous ones that you must learn to recognize.

Wild strawberries, wild raspberries, blueberries, and blackberries are all delicious. Cloudberries, which grow in boggy moorlands, are more rare. Some people say that they are the best of all.

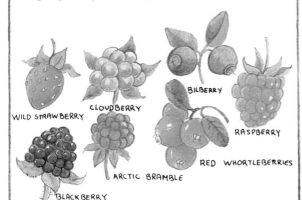

WILD STRAWBERRY
CLOUDBERRY
BILBERRY
RASPBERRY
ARCTIC BRAMBLE
RED WHORTLEBERRIES
BLACKBERRY

Red whortleberries ripen in the autumn. Most berries can be eaten fresh, but rowan berries are best if they are made into a jelly.

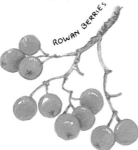

ROWAN BERRIES

Have you tried threading wild strawberries on a piece of grass? If you place an unripe berry at the bottom, the rest won't fall off.

GOOD LEAVES

Leaves can be used to make tea. They are dried and then crumbled. Many plants make good teas: birch, wild strawberry, rosebay, and meadow-sweets. From the garden: black currant, strawberry, apple and pear leaves. Fir and pine-tree needles can also be used for tea. Crush fresh needles in a mortar.

... OR ELSE I'D HAVE GOT A TUMMY ACHE!

FLOWERS

Small woodland mammals

What is a mammal?

Most animals' body temperature varies according to the outside temperature, but birds and mammals have more or less the same temperature all the time; they are warm-blooded.

Mammals give birth to living young, which are fed on their mother's milk. They have hair on their bodies (some less than others — for example, human beings), and usually four legs.

Rodents are an important source of food for many larger animals and birds of prey. In years when there are many rodents, there are more beasts of prey, too. Most rodents, such as rats, mice, and the gray squirrel, are small, but the beaver is also a rodent.

Some common mammals

Field voles live mostly in meadows. During

THE FIELD VOLE HAS A SHORT TAIL...   ...WHILE THE FIELD MOUSE HAS A LONG TAIL

Whales, which aren't fish, as some people think, have no legs at all.

Here are some small mammals that you and Nicky might see:

Rodents

Most of the many mammals in the woods and fields are rodents. They have only two front teeth in their upper jaw.

particularly cold winters, they make long tunnels under the snow and line them with dried grass. Nicky sometimes finds these grass baskets on the ground when the snow has melted.

All voles have quite short tails.

The field mouse comes out mostly at night. It lives at the edge of woods or in thickets, and eats seeds, nuts, and acorns. Sometimes it will

26

MY GUINEA PIG IS A RODENT, TOO

PLEASE GOD, LET ME SEE A SHREW!

spend the winter in a warm house.

The house mouse is a little smaller than the field mouse and lives indoors. Even the brown rat comes inside, but it isn't welcome.

The shrew is not a rodent

Shrews look like small mice but are related to moles. They have long, pointy noses and are easier to hear than to see. If you hear a squeaking in the grass, it is probably a shrew. Shrews include the smallest mammals; they can be less than five centimeters (two inches) long, excluding their tails.

The hare and the rabbit

Hares and rabbits have teeth like rodents, but they aren't closely related to them. Hares and rabbits produce droppings, which can be seen all over their territory, especially around rabbit warrens. They pass two kinds. We see only the second. The first dropping is greenish and is eaten by the rabbit or hare, as it contains vitamins.

THIS IS WHAT A SHREW LOOKS LIKE

I HOPE THIS DOESN'T HURT THE EARTHWORM

It's wonderful to lie on your stomach on a little dock and peer down into the water. There are lots of small fish and animals to see.

Make an underwater viewer just like Nicky's. Take a large metal can and remove the top and the bottom. Place the can in a clear plastic bag and put a strong rubber band around it near the top, to hold it tight. Place the bottom in the water and look through the open end. The plastic will bend a little like a magnifying glass.

I'VE MADE AN UNDERWATER VIEWER

In this picture, you can see Nicky fishing. It's fun to fish in the rain because the fish bite a lot. Does it hurt the earthworm when you put it on the hook? Apparently not. No one has ever been able to find a sense organ for pain in an earthworm.

Right away you get a bite and up comes a perch. On its back it has sharp fins to defend itself against other fish that might try to eat it.

You can see how a fish breathes. Behind its mouth, at the sides of its head, are the gills. They are hidden behind gill covers.

The fish breathes/gulps water in through its open mouth. It closes its mouth and squeezes out the water through its gills. The gills take in the oxygen from the water that the fish needs to breathe.

In front of the back fin, beneath the body, there is a little hole. This is where the fish's droppings come out into the water. They fall on the bottom and are changed into fertilizer for the plants.

28

At the water's edge

Plants along the bank

Reeds grow along the edge of ponds and streams, where the water is full of nutrients. The common reed is a type of grass. It can grow to five meters (sixteen feet) in height, but it usually stands a meter (three feet) deep in water.

Cattail, with its brown "cigars," grows along with the common reed. Those strange cigars are really flowers. Each cigar can have more than one hundred thousand tiny flowers on it.

In late winter, the cigars burst and release masses of winged fruits over the water.

... and animals

The water is teeming with animals. Snails crawl beneath the surface. Whirligig beetles swim with circular movements on the water's surface; they look as if they are skating. Whirligig beetles have divided eyes; the upper one remains above the water, and the lower one remains below.

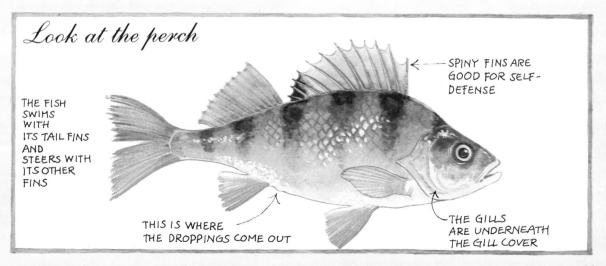

Look at the perch

SPINY FINS ARE GOOD FOR SELF-DEFENSE

THE FISH SWIMS WITH ITS TAIL FINS AND STEERS WITH ITS OTHER FINS

THIS IS WHERE THE DROPPINGS COME OUT

THE GILLS ARE UNDERNEATH THE GILL COVER

29

The life of a dragonfly

Nicky wishes that she could fly like a dragonfly. It's amazing. It can hover, fly backward, or glide. You can hear its wings rustling when they bump into each other. There are many kinds of dragonflies, each more beautiful than the other. The backs of their bodies have especially striking markings.

While they are mating, two dragonflies can fly attached together. The male attaches the tip

of his tail beneath the female's head, and she bends her tail forward onto the male's body where he has his mating organs.

When they have mated, she lays her eggs. Some dragonflies drop them into the water while they are flying, but others lay their eggs in moss or damp earth on land. Others crawl into the water and attach their eggs to plants underneath the surface.

It takes the larvae of some types of dragonflies several years to become adults. The larva crawls up out of the water onto a reed. Its skin splits down the back, and the dragonfly pulls itself out. Its old larval skin remains on the stalk. Its wings unfold and dry; then it flies away. It lives only a couple of months.

Dragonflies hunt small flying insects. They have small territories, just as birds do.

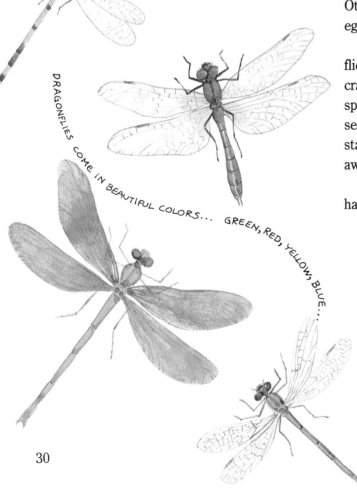

DRAGONFLIES COME IN BEAUTIFUL COLORS... GREEN, RED, YELLOW, BLUE...

AUTUMN

This is the weather the shepherd shuns,
  And so do I;
When beeches drip in browns and duns,
  And thresh, and ply;
And hill-hid tides throb, throe on throe,
And meadow rivulets overflow,
And drops on gate-bars hang in a row,
And rooks in families homeward go,
  And so do I.

Thomas Hardy

TREES

The maple leaves have turned brilliant shades of yellow, orange, and red. Nicky presses and dries some leaves and makes pictures with them. The large black spots that sometimes appear on the leaves are fungus. Can you see any "helicopters" left on the tree?

BIRDS

Starlings are in their winter outfits; they no longer have the shiny spots that they had in the spring. Swallows sit on the telephone wires, resting on their way south. Squawking, the blackbird gets ready to join a flock of blackbirds; most migrant birds travel in groups.

PLANTS

The celandine leaves are dark green and have started to wither around the edges; the hedgerows are bright with orange rosehips and dark red hawthorn berries. Most flowers have withered and disappeared.

INSECTS

The peacock and the small tortoiseshell butterfly are both still about, but soon they will look for a place to take shelter for the winter. Except for a few lazy wasps, there aren't very many insects left.

OTHER ANIMALS

When it grows colder, the grass is wet with dew in the morning. Suddenly you can see all the spiders' webs, those treacherous traps for insects. Slugs and garden snails are still crawling about.

A field vole rustles in the grass. It had better watch out for the buzzard, who is very fond of voles!

What happens to seeds and

What is a fruit and what is a seed? Well, a fruit is the part of the flower that contains the seed. Some fruits, such as strawberries and raspberries, are soft and taste good. The crunchy bits are the seeds. Other fruits, such as hazelnuts, beechnuts, and sweet chestnuts, are hard, although you can eat what's inside them. Deer like beechnuts, and squirrels bury hoards of acorns.

How are seeds spread?
The wind scatters seeds very effectively. Blow a dandelion "clock" so that the seeds sail through the air like parachutes, each with a tiny pilot hanging below.

Animals help to disperse seeds, too. Birds, such as blackbirds and starlings, eat soft fruits. The seeds come out in their droppings. Animals can get seeds with hooks or burrs stuck on their fur: dogs come home with burdocks on them. Ants carry off small seeds and help to spread them, too.

Why do trees and shrubs lose their leaves in autumn?
Leaves give out water vapor through their tiny holes all the time. In the winter, when the ground is frozen, trees and shrubs get very little water through the roots. If the leaves remained, the tree might lose all its water and die.

What about fir and pine trees, then? Their leaves — needles — remain throughout the winter. But needles are narrow and covered with a waxy coating, so less water escapes from them.

What happens when a leaf falls off?
The tree seals up the area where the leaf stalk was attached to the branch, so that neither water nor insects nor fungus can enter. (In the

where do all the leaves go?

picture of the horse chestnut on pages fourteen and fifteen, you can see this triangular leaf scar.)

Where do all the leaves go?

There are masses of leaves. A football field covered with leaves would weigh about one thousand kilos (2,200 pounds). But, by spring, most of them have disappeared. Where do they go?

Earthworms dispose of a lot of them. They drag them down into their tunnels under the ground and eat them. Earthworms are more interesting than you think. Nicky likes to listen to them. Try it yourself! Let an earthworm crawl across a piece of paper and you will hear the scratching of its tiny bristles. If you use a magnifying glass, you can see them clearly. The earthworm uses its bristles to brace itself against the walls of its tunnels. When a blackbird pulls a worm up out of the ground, you can see the worm stretching out — it is holding on with its bristles.

DO YOU KNOW WHAT I FOUND IN A LITTLE SQUARE THIS BIG IN THE WOODS?

LISTEN!

It's not only earthworms that eat leaves. In a ten centimeter (four inch) square of a woodland floor, Nicky found:

3 SLUGS
14 MILLIPEDES
23 INSECTS AND THEIR LARVAE
120 BIG EARTHWORMS
217 WOOD LICE
635 SPIDERS
63,000 TINY WORMS
30,000,000 BACTERIA

If these creatures covered a whole football field, they would weigh about five thousand kilos (11,000 pounds). It's not surprising that all the dead leaves disappear before spring comes.

35

Insy winsy spider

It's amazing how many people dislike spiders. They think spiders are poisonous and that they bite. It is true that they are dangerous for flies and insects, but people don't have to worry. Some spiders spin fine webs, but most don't make any webs at all. They either chase their prey or ambush it from behind.

Spiders and webs

Autumn is the best time to see spiders' webs. When the meadow is wet with dew, Nicky can see all the different webs stretched between the bushes and the blades of grass. Some look like wheels; others are like thick covers. When the dew dries up, you can't see the webs anymore. They really are death traps for insects.

Spiders have spinnerets on the undersides of their bodies. They start by spinning a frame. There are sticky strands for catching careless insects and dry ones for the spider to travel along.

Only the female spider spins a web. She has a kind of oil on her feet so that she won't get caught in her own web.

Spiderweb thread is very thin, only 1/200 of a millimeter thick, but it is made up of many strands and is therefore very strong.

The spider's courtship

The female spider is nearly always hungry. She sees every animal that approaches her web as a possible meal. Even male spiders that come to mate with her. The male must make sure she is in a good mood, or he'll be eaten up. Some types of spiders mate with no problems. The male vibrates the web, which attracts the female. Among other types, the male ties up the bigger and stronger female before he mates with her, just to be safe.

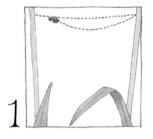

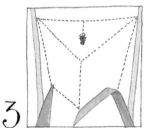

THIS IS HOW A SPIDER SPINS ITS WEB BETWEEN THE BLADES OF GRASS

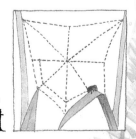

Spiders can fly

But they don't have wings. In the autumn, the spiderlings journey through the air. They sit on a branch and spin a long thread, which catches the wind. It is like a voyage in a balloon, where the spider can adjust the height by letting out more thread or taking it in. If it is very windy, the wind carries the young spiders far away. In this way, spiders have journeyed all over the world and spread to new areas.

Animals

How do animals survive the winter? The weather can grow very cold, and there is little food available. Some birds travel, or migrate, to warmer climates, while other animals go to sleep, or into hibernation. Animals which are staying through the winter gather food and store it away to eat later. They also grow thick coats to help keep them warm. Some insects spend the winter underneath tree bark. Others, before they die, lay eggs that survive the winter.

When an animal hibernates, its temperature drops and it breathes so slowly that you hardly notice it.

The badger does not hibernate. In bad weather, it goes to sleep in its labyrinth of underground tunnels deep in the ground. Sometimes, generations of badgers have lived in the same burrow. If the weather grows mild, the badger wakes up and goes out for a ramble.

The bear also dozes in a winter den. It gives birth to its young in the den during the winter.

Animals which doze in winter hideouts breathe normally and retain their usual body temperature. They can be waked up immediately, although they might be in a bad mood. There's an old saying, "Never wake a sleeping bear."

Mice and voles gather a store of food throughout the autumn: nuts, acorns, apple seeds, and grains of corn are put away in holes in the ground. They don't sleep in winter but scamper about, even under the snow. You can often spot their tracks in the snow.

The hare's fur grows thicker in winter, but it remains brown all year round.

Birds which don't migrate must hunt for food all day long. The days grow shorter and colder, and the nights colder still. Many small birds die. They freeze to death or starve. Nicky sets up a bird table in the garden for them.

Snakes, frogs, and toads look for a safe place to hide away from the frost. Deep in the ground or under a pile of wood, toads wait for the warmth of spring.

Frogs often bury themselves in the mud at the bottom of a pond. They take in oxygen from the water through their skins.

Sometimes you can find adders and grass snakes curled up in a burrow together.

The ladybird hides itself in a crack in a tree, a tuft of grass, or among leaves. It isn't fussy.

You can find peacock and small tortoiseshell butterflies in attics, cellars, and woodsheds.

They sleep with folded wings. Crickets and grasshoppers die before winter comes, but they have already laid their eggs, which will grow into new insects in the spring.

Snails retreat to a sheltered, frost-free place. They produce a foam made of lime at the opening of their shells. It hardens and seals the entrance so that they don't dry out. Slugs, which don't have shells, lay their eggs in the autumn and then die. The eggs hatch in the spring and the new slugs appear in the summer.

Why do birds migrate?

There are 645 types of birds in North America. The birds that eat insects need to go elsewhere in the cold season when the insects die; otherwise, they would starve to death.

But birds usually don't wait until the insects have disappeared before they depart. They set off far earlier. Birds, like animals and people, have chemicals called hormones in their bodies. The amount of hormones changes when the days grow shorter and the temperature lower. This change makes the birds eat all the time, storing fat in their bodies for the exhausting migration ahead. Then they set off. In the spring, when the birds fly northward again, their sex glands produce new hormones. Sometimes we say that birds have a "body clock" that tells them when to migrate.

Birds take quite a long time to travel to the south. Most of them fly at night. They use the daytime to look for food. Swallows and swifts fly with open mouths and catch insects while they are flying. When the birds return in the spring, they travel much more quickly.

Bird ringing

How do we know where birds migrate? Well, some scientists catch birds, place tiny aluminium rings, saying where the bird was caught and when, around their legs, and release them. If you find a dead bird with a ring, you should send it to the address on the ring. This is how scientists who study birds learn where they migrate.

Nesting boxes

Autumn is a good time to put up new nesting boxes and empty out the old ones. Make sure that all the boxes are securely fastened. Nicky

Which birds migrate and which ones stay behind?

Sparrows
STAY WITH US ALL YEAR ROUND

Robins
ARE PERMANENT RESIDENTS

Wagtails
MIGRATE TO THE MEDITERRANEAN

Swallows
FLY ALL THE WAY TO SOUTHERN AFRICA

puts a little moss in the nesting box, which makes it more comfortable for birds staying overnight.

Build a nesting box yourself. Take a piece of wood about two centimeters (three-fourths of an inch) thick and thirteen centimeters (five inches) wide. Saw it as shown in the drawing below.

Screw a support on the back of the box so you can fasten it to a tree. Drill a hole about 3.5 centimeters (1.5 inches) in diameter on the front. Arrange the pieces together to see if they fit, and screw and glue them together. (You may need help!) This box would suit a robin, a tyrant flycatcher, or a redstart.

Don't put a perch in front of the hole — this makes it easier for a cat to get at the young. Place nesting boxes facing south and east, and not too close together.

You can, of course, buy a nesting box instead.

SEE YOU AGAIN NEXT YEAR...

Building a nesting box isn't so difficult with the help of an adult. You take a piece of wood 150 centimeters (five feet) long and saw it like this . . .

HOLE

|←—30—→|←—28—→|←—30—→|←—28—→|←10→|←—24—→|

| SIDE | SIDE | BACK | O FRONT | FLOOR | ROOF |

|←———————————————150———————————————→|

WINTER

Winter morning

Winter is the king of showmen,
Turning tree stumps into snow men
And houses into birthday cakes
And spreading sugar over lakes.
Smooth and clean and frosty white,
The world looks good enough to bite.
That's the season to be young,
Catching snowflakes on your tongue.
Snow is snowy when it's snowing
I'm sorry it's slushy when it's going.

Ogden Nash

TREES

The leaves have long since fallen off the maple tree, but there are still a few "helicopters" here and there. Snow lies on some of the bigger branches. The tree is resting for the winter and is well provided for.

BIRDS

A blackbird sits on a low branch of the maple tree. A nuthatch searches the cracks in the tree's bark for insects. Sparrows can always be found, but there aren't many other birds about.

PLANTS

Most plants have withered. Only the dry stalk of cow parsley remains. The burdock is brown. Its prickly fruits release their seeds in the winter for the birds to eat.

INSECTS

There are insects hiding in cracks in the bark of the maple and other trees, and the birds hunt for them eagerly. It is rare to see an insect outside.

OTHER ANIMALS

The hare leaps over the snow in its brown fur. It is easy to spot and has no protection apart from its speed.

Mice, voles, and shrews live under the snow. Sometimes you can find the tracks on the snow.

This is how a mouse eats: It is a neat eater. The cone is stripped clean and only the core remains.

This is how a squirrel eats: It holds the pine-cone tightly and gnaws both scales and seeds. The cone looks a bit sloppy.

This is how a woodpecker eats: It pecks violently at the cones to pick out the seeds. The cones get totally demolished.

HARE

DEER

TYPICAL HARE DROPPINGS!

Nicky has learned to identify the tracks of different animals, as well as other signs such as droppings and food remains. Animals leave behind all sorts of clues, even in winter. Many animals eat pine-cones, and you can tell who has eaten them by the remains. Wood-peckers wedge their cones into a crack in a tree before eating them. Beneath the tree there are usually large piles of cones that have fallen down. You can find hazelnuts with

...AND WHO'S DONE A POO HERE?

FOX

SQUIRREL

MOOSE

large holes in them wedged in cracks in a tree.

Mice and voles make neat round holes in nuts with clear teeth marks.

Squirrels crack nuts in half and leave the shell behind.

Feet leave tracks

Hare tracks are easy to spot. Hares hide in their open nests, called forms, in the daytime. They make clear footprints, and you can get quite close to one before it runs away. Rabbit tracks are the same as hare's, but smaller.

Fox prints wind through the fields and along ditches. Dog and fox tracks are quite alike.

Squirrels leave tracks on the ground when it's too far to hop between the trees.

You can see the drag marks of a rodent's tail between its footprints. The moose leaves clear footprints; those belonging to the deer are smaller. Nicky spots hare droppings here and there. Moose and deer droppings look like the hare's, but they are larger.

The fox leaves its dropping on top of a rock or tree stump. It is less likely to be surprised by an enemy there.

SOMETIMES YOU'RE LUCKY

Plants,

taking in twigs of birch or hazel. Start in early January and continue picking a twig a week throughout the winter. The first branches won't do anything, but eventually you will see the buds start to open.

Look at the wasp's nest

Nicky has taken down the wasp's nest in the attic. Next year's wasps will build a new one, anyway. They are beautifully built, with different stories and with columns in between. The nest is light but strong. It is made of chewed-up wood — just like papier mâché.

When the wind blows hard, the birds stand on the ice with their beaks facing the wind. Their feathers are pressed against their bodies so that no cold air can get through. Otherwise, the wind would ruffle their feathers and squeeze out the warm air next to their bodies. They would freeze.

Don't their feet freeze?

Birds have very few blood vessels in their legs. They can close some of them off if it gets too cold. Then there isn't so much blood to cool down.

Most plants wither away in winter, but their roots live on underground. Other plants lose their leaves. Only the evergreens provide color against the snow. Pine trees survive well because their leaves are covered with waxy layers. Nicky scratches a pineneedle with her nail and looks at it under a magnifying glass.

Under the snow, the buds are ready for next year's flowering.

Why don't flowers bloom?

Sometimes in the middle of winter there are warm, sunny days, but the flowers still don't blossom.

All plants need a winter's rest before the buds can start to develop. You can test this by

animals and winter

The owl
hunts at night. It can see very well even in little light, but it hears even better. No rodent moving under the snow is safe. Suddenly, the owl pounces.

Owls fly silently because their wing feathers are fringed on the outer edge and the air filters through the fringes.

Bees keep each other warm
Bees spend the winter in their hives. They huddle together to keep warm. If it gets too cold, they fan their wings, which increases the heat. The temperature in the hive never goes below 12°C. (54 F.) even in a truly cold winter.

Animals under the snow
A thick blanket of snow is the best protection against cold that either an animal or a plant can have. In the space between the snow and the ground, the temperature is near zero degrees Centigrade (32 F.).

Take some leaves home!
Nicky digs underneath the snow and takes home a bag full of dead leaves. She places them on a tray. At first, nothing stirs, but after a while the small animals wake up. The leaf litter is teeming with life!

OH ME! OH MY!

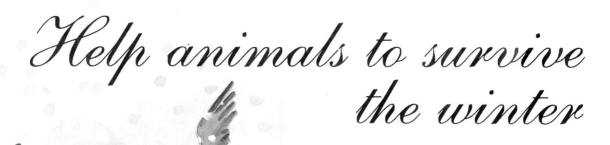

Help animals to survive the winter

HELP YOURSELVES!
TEA'S READY!

If the winter is hard, animals have a difficult time. Many birds look to people to get food. Why don't you make a bird table for them?

On the table, put sunflower seeds and oats, not just bread crusts. The bread should not be moldy.

Melt some suet or fat, together with chopped nuts, sunflower seeds, and grain. When it has cooled, place the mixture in net bags (onion or potato sacks would work well) and hang them in a tree or bush. Put apples under the bird table — the blackbirds (and mice!) will love them. In the autumn, Nicky picked bunches of rowan berries and kept them in her freezer. Now that it is cold and there is little food, she hangs them from twigs for the birds.

Try making a simple seed dispenser. Cut some holes in the side of a plastic bucket near the bottom. Place it on a tree stump. (To get a larger dining table, you could hammer a piece of plywood, or an old tray, on the stump.) Put a lid on the bucket to keep the rain out. A bucket full of seeds will last for two weeks.

But, remember! If you have started giving the animals food, you must continue until spring comes.

It's very exciting to watch all the birds. Nicky has seen house sparrows, tree sparrows, goldfinches, house finches, and blackbirds. What have *you* seen?

DO YOU WANT TO READ FURTHER?

Try your local library. You'll find all kinds of nature books. Just ask the librarian. Here are a few examples:

Wildflowers and the Stories Behind Their Names
by Phyllis S. Busch. New York: Charles Scribner's Sons, 1977.

Getting Started in Bird Watching
by Edward W. Cronin, Jr. Boston: Houghton Mifflin, 1986.

A Practical Guide for the Amateur Naturalist
by Gerald Durrell. New York: Alfred A. Knopf, 1983.

The Cambridge Illustrated Dictionary of Natural History
by R. J. Lincoln and G. A. Boxshall. New York: Cambridge University Press, 1987.

Bugs
by Nancy Winslow Parker and Joan Richards Wright. New York: Greenwillow, 1987.

Do Animals Dream: Children's questions about animals most often asked of the Museum of Natural History
by Joyce Pope. New York: Viking Penguin, 1986.

The Evolution Book
by Sara Stein. New York: Workman, 1986.